Zoomer Field Notes

Teeth

goatrilla

polar cow

dogephant

shicken pigcock

norsodile libbit

shiger

horsodile

Poo

libbit

norsodile

duckaroo

shicken

shiger

polar cow

pigcock

goatrilla

givapooster

dogephant

Hair/feathers/scales

goatrilla

polar cow

shiger

shicken

horsodile

pigcock

dogephant

givapooster

libbit

For Tom,
the original zoomer.

American edition published in 2016 by Andersen Press USA,
an imprint of Andersen Press Ltd.
www.andersenpressusa.com

First published in Great Britain in 2015 by Andersen Press Ltd.,
20 Vauxhall Bridge Road, London SW1V 2SA.

Distributed in the United States and Canada by
Lerner Publishing Group, Inc.
241 First Avenue North
Minneapolis, MN 55401 USA
For reading levels and more information, look up this title at www.lernerbooks.com.
Printed and bound in Malaysia by Tien Wah Press.

Library of Congress Cataloging-in-Publication Data Available.
ISBN:978-1-5124-0424-1
1-TWP-6/1/15

The ZOOMERS' Handbook

Ana & Thiago de Moraes

ANDERSEN PRESS USA

This is *not* a handbook for zookeepers.

Zookeepers look after monkeys, elephants, and lions. That's easy.

This is *not* a handbook for farmers.

Farmers look after chickens, cows, and pigs.
Anyone can do that.

This is a handbook for *Zoomers*.
Zoomers look after very special beasts . . .

Take the goatrilla for example. He likes to climb and he likes to swing from trees. Remember to feed him at least 10 cans of bananas a day. He loves to eat cans.

This is the polar cow, a very practical animal. If you feed it strawberries and get it to dance around before milking time, it makes ice cream!

The shiger
is grandma's
favorite
animal.
Its stripey
wool makes
the nicest
sweaters.

The shicken lays delicious eggs,

but letting it eat corn from your hand is not a good idea.

The horsodile is the best ride when you need

to get somewhere fast, even if it's underwater.

The pigcock is one of the most beautiful animals on earth—at least in theory.

Few people have seen its feathers, as they are often covered in mud.

The dogephant
loves to play.
But don't let it
jump on you—
it weighs a ton.

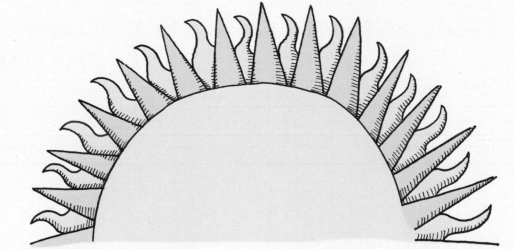

The girafooster will get you up bright and early. It spots the sun

from way up high, as soon as it starts to rise.

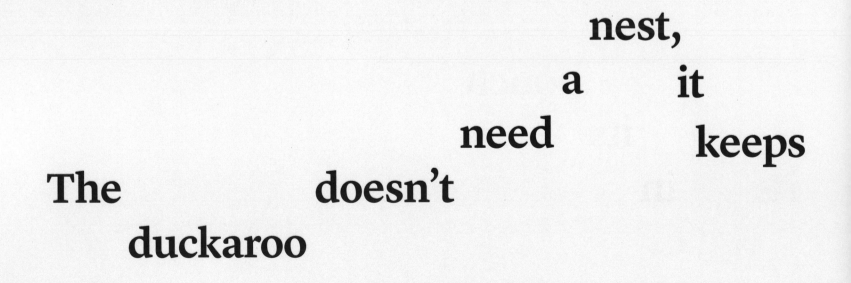

The duckaroo doesn't need a nest, it keeps

its
eggs
its   in
its
pouch
instead.

Finally, beware of the libbit: it may be small,

but it likes to be treated like a king.

**Now that you've met all the animals,
you know what it takes to be a Zoomer.**

It's time to get to work!